Disney

VILLAINS

MALEFICENT

WITHDRAWN

Written by
Steve Behling
Illustrated by the
Disney Storybook Art Team

SUSTAINABLE
FORESTRY
INITIATIVE
Certified Sourcing
www.sfiprogram.org
SFI-01415

Welcome, my friend!
I see you have entered the forest.
It is only a short walk
to where I live.

See this castle?
It belongs to me.
You must cross a rickety
bridge to get there.

When you arrive,
a stone raven will come to life.
The Raven will say, "Caw! Caw!"
He will tell me that I have a guest.

Who am I?

Why, I am Maleficent, of course.

I am a very powerful fairy.

How powerful am I, you ask?

Sit back, and I will tell you.

I can do all kinds of magic.
For example, I talk to birds.
They obey my every word.

I also have many helpers.
They are creatures who
do anything I ask.
If I tell them to scare someone,
they will!

Today my pet raven tells me about a party at the king's castle. "Why was I not invited?" I wonder. Perhaps I shall go for a visit!

My magic lets me travel
anywhere.

In a flash of green fire,

I appear inside the king's castle.

Everyone is scared of me.

That is just the way I like it!

"Why did you not invite me?" I ask.

The king orders me to leave.

Who does he think he is?

I will show this king who is

really in charge.

Then the king orders his guards
to capture me.
Simple guards catching
the most powerful fairy?
I laugh and cast an evil spell.

In a flash of green fire,
everyone turns to stone.
The people at the party
have become statues!

"If anyone does not wish me
to be here, speak up." I laugh.
No one says anything, of course.
Statues cannot talk!
You know, I can be funny.

I soon grow bored of my trick.

I reverse the spell.

Everyone is back to normal.

But if you thought they
were afraid of me before,
look at them now!

What a fun party!
I am so glad that I went.
But now it is time for me
to go home.
I have something important to do.

You see, before I left the party,
I played *another* trick.
I brought someone to my castle.
Who is it, you ask?

Oh, just a little prince.

I tell him that I will set him free.

But his father has to invite me

to every royal party!

The prince is not happy.

The prince escapes from my prison!
But I can change into a fearsome
fire-breathing dragon.
Just let the prince try to get past *me*!

I chase the prince to the edge of
a cliff.

He has a shield and a sword.

I am a mighty dragon.

He does not stand a chance!

I allow the prince to leave.
He will tell his father
to invite me to every party.
Now I wish to tell you a secret.

I do not want to go to every party.
I do not want to go to *any* parties!
I just do not like it when
people do not invite me to parties.

It is time for you to leave.
Goodbye . . . until next time!

5